Jr. Graphic Mysteries™

UFOs

The Roswell Incident

Jack DeMolay

PowerKiDS press™

New York

Published in 2007 by The Rosen Publishing Group, Inc.
29 East 21st Street, New York, NY 10010

First Edition

Editor: Jennifer Way
Book Design: Ginny Chu
Illustrations: Q2A

Library of Congress Cataloging-in-Publication Data

DeMolay, Jack.
  UFOs : the Roswell incident / by Jack DeMolay.— 1st ed.
      p. cm. — (Jr. graphic mysteries)
  Includes index.
  ISBN (10) 1-4042-3403-9 — (13) 978-1-4042-3403-1 (library binding) — ISBN (10) 1-4042-2156-5 — (13) 978-1-4042-2156-7 (pbk)
  1. Unidentified flying objects—Juvenile literature. I. Title. II. Series.
  TL789.2.D46 2007
  001.94209789'43—dc22
                                    2005037335

Manufactured in the United States of America

Contents

UFOs:

 The Roswell Incident 4

Did You Know? 22

Glossary 23

Index and Web Sites 24

UFOS: THE ROSWELL INCIDENT

IT WAS SUMMER 1947.

THE PLACE WAS ROSWELL, NEW MEXICO.

IT WAS A STRANGE TIME IN AMERICA.

STORIES OF THE UNKNOWN WERE RUNNING WILD.

LOOK, PA! DO YOU SEE IT?

WHAT IS IT, DAN?

PEOPLE HAD BEEN CLAIMING THEY HAD LOOKED UP INTO THE NIGHT SKY AND SEEN SOMETHING.

ACCORDING TO EYEWITNESS REPORTS, A UFO MAY HAVE CRASHED OUTSIDE OF ROSWELL ON JUNE 14, 1947.

NOW WHAT ON EARTH IS THAT?

RANCHER MACK BRAZEL WAS THE FIRST TO SEE THE STRANGE **WRECKAGE**.

THE WRECKAGE DID NOT SEEM TO COME FROM EARTH.

BRAZEL ALSO SAW A LONG RUT LEADING AWAY FROM THE WRECKAGE.

MACK BRAZEL WASN'T THE ONLY PERSON TO SEE A UFO THAT SUMMER.

I HEAR THEY'RE GIVING OUT **REWARDS** FOR ANYONE WHO CAN PROVE THEY HAVE SEEN A UFO!

BRAZEL RETURNED WITH HIS FAMILY TO RECOVER THE WRECKAGE.

WOW!

YOU SHOULD SHOW THIS TO THE **SHERIFF**.

Police
Station

YOU SAW
A UFO?

BRAZEL WENT TO THE SHERIFF.

HELLO,
MAJOR? I HAVE SOME
NEWS YOU MIGHT FIND
INTERESTING.

SOON THE ARMY ARRIVED.

THE ARMY SET OUT FOR THE DESERT TO VIEW THE STRANGE WRECKAGE.

MAJOR JESSE MARCEL WAS THE ARMY OFFICER IN CHARGE OF THE OPERATION.

LOOKS LIKE SOMETHING **EXPLODED** ABOVE THE GROUND AND FELL.

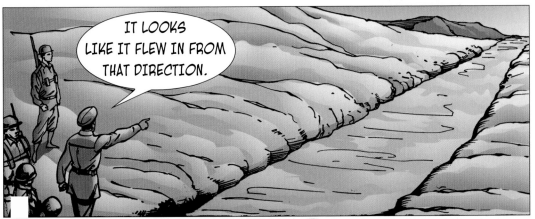

IT LOOKS LIKE IT FLEW IN FROM THAT DIRECTION.

THEN IT LANDED HERE.

IT WAS A MYSTERY THAT GREW BY THE MINUTE.

WHERE DID THE UFO COME FROM?

WHY DID IT CRASH?

WAS IT FROM OUTER SPACE?

THE ARMY BEGAN TO CLEAR THE WRECKAGE.

THEY BROUGHT IT TO THE ROSWELL ARMY AIRFIELD BASE.

MAJOR MARCEL DROVE HOME TO SHOW HIS FAMILY A FEW PIECES OF THE WRECKAGE.

JESSE, WHAT IS THAT?

YOU JUST WOULDN'T BELIEVE IT, HONEY.

WHAT IS IT, DAD?

I-I DON'T KNOW, SON.

I'VE SEEN ALL SORTS OF AIRPLANES, ROCKETS, EVEN **WEATHER BALLOONS.**

THIS ISN'T ANY OF THOSE THINGS.

THE NEXT DAY THE LOCAL NEWSPAPER SEEMED TO AGREE WITH MARCEL'S CLAIMS.

DAILY RECO

R.A.A.F. CAPTURES UFO IN ROSWELL AREA

SO, IT'S TRUE? UFOS EXIST?

YEAH, THE ARMY FOUND IT!

DOES THAT MEAN THEY FOUND **ALIENS?**

WAIT, FELLAS! COME QUICK! LISTEN TO THIS!

THE ARMY IS NOW REPORTING THAT WHAT THEY FOUND WAS A WEATHER BALLOON AND NOT A UFO.

WHAT? A WEATHER BALLOON?

THE ARMY HAD CHANGED THEIR STORY WITHIN HOURS.

WAS THE ARMY AFRAID THAT THE PUBLIC WOULD LEARN THE TRUTH?

A WEATHER BALLOON? THAT'S NOT WHAT I FOUND IN THAT FIELD!

PEOPLE LIKE MACK BRAZEL REFUSED TO BELIEVE THE WRECKAGE WAS ANYTHING BUT A UFO.

ARMY CREWS CONTINUED TO CLEAN UP THE WRECKAGE.

LOCAL PEOPLE WONDERED WHY SO MUCH ATTENTION WAS BEING PAID TO A WEATHER BALLOON CRASH.

THIS AREA IS RESTRICTED.

I THINK THE ARMY'S HIDING SOMETHING.

TALK OF AN ARMY COVER-UP SPREAD THROUGH TOWN. SOON THE ROSWELL MYSTERY TOOK ANOTHER TURN.

BALLARD FUNERAL HOME

MEANWHILE, AT THE BALLARD **FUNERAL** HOME, GLENN DENNIS RECEIVED A PHONE CALL.

YES, HELLO?

YOU WANT WHAT?

THE ARMY BASE ASKED DENNIS FOR SEVERAL SMALL **COFFINS.**

COULD THE COFFINS HAVE BEEN FOR DEAD ALIENS?

LATER THAT NIGHT DENNIS VISITED THE ARMY BASE.

THIS BASE IS RESTRICTED.

DENNIS MET A NURSE FROM THE ARMY BASE IN SECRET.

WHAT I'M ABOUT TO TELL YOU IS TOP SECRET, MR. DENNIS.

THE NURSE SAID SHE HAD SEEN SEVERAL ALIEN **AUTOPSIES**!

ALIENS?

WHATEVER THEY WERE, THEY WEREN'T HUMAN.

PLEASE KEEP THIS A SECRET. MY LIFE DEPENDS ON IT.

YOU HAVE MY WORD.

THE STRANGE EVENTS FOLLOWING THE CRASH IN ROSWELL DID NOT END THERE.

WEEKS LATER A LOCAL FIRE DEPARTMENT CLAIMED TO HAVE FOUND SOMETHING UNUSUAL AT THE CRASH **SITE**.

IT WAS A SMALL OBJECT THAT FLOATED IN THE AIR BY ITSELF!

THE FIREMEN WERE SOON FORCED TO GIVE UP THE OBJECT TO THE ARMY.

THE SOLDIERS WHO TOOK PART IN THE CLEANUP WERE TOLD TO FORGET IT HAPPENED.

ALMOST EVERY ARMY EYEWITNESS TO THE CRASH EITHER **TRANSFERRED** OR DISAPPEARED!

MOST REPORTS STATED THAT THE WRECKAGE FROM THE CRASH SITE WAS TAKEN TO A SECRET MILITARY BASE IN OHIO.

THESE REPORTS GAVE RISE TO THE **LEGEND** OF **HANGAR** 18.

IT IS SAID THAT ALIENS AND UFOS ARE SECRETLY KEPT THERE.

SOME PEOPLE BELIEVE THE ROSWELL WRECKAGE WAS BROUGHT TO A SECRET ARMY BASE IN NEVADA CALLED AREA 51.

AREA 51 IS ONE OF THE MOST HEAVILY GUARDED BASES IN THE WORLD.

ARE THEY HIDING SOMETHING FROM THE PUBLIC? WHAT IS IN THERE?

UFOS?

ALIENS?

AS LONG AS THERE ARE PEOPLE WHO IMAGINE AND DREAM, THERE WILL BE STORIES OF ALIENS AND UFOS.

THERE! DID YOU SEE IT?

IS THERE LIFE ON OTHER **PLANETS?** HAVE ALIENS VISITED EARTH?

WE MAY NEVER KNOW FOR SURE.

THE END

Did You Know?

- Area 51 has had many different names over the years, including Groom Lake, Dreamland, Paradise Ranch, Watertown Strip, the Box, and the Pig Farm.

- Some reports claim that the secret base at Area 51 has as many as 22 levels below ground.

- The land area of Area 51 and the air force base that surrounds it is roughly the size of the state of Connecticut.

- The U.S. government has never officially stated that Area 51 exists.

Glossary

aliens (AY-lee-unz) Creatures from outer space.

autopsies (AH-top-seez) Operations done on dead bodies to find out the cause of death.

coffins (KAH-finz) Boxes that hold dead bodies.

exploded (ek-SPLOHD-ed) Blew up.

funeral (FYOON-rul) The service held when burying the dead.

hangar (HANG-er) A large building where airplanes are stored.

legend (LEH-jend) A story, passed down through the years, that cannot be proved.

planets (PLA-nets) Large objects, such as Earth, that move around the Sun.

rancher (RANCH-ir) A person who works on a large farm for raising cattle, horses, or sheep.

restricted (rih-STRIKT-ed) Kept within limits.

rewards (rih-WARDZ) Prizes, usually money, given to people for doing something.

sheriff (SHER-if) The head law officer of a county.

site (SYT) The place where a certain event happens.

transferred (TRANS-ferd) Moved to a different location.

unidentified (un-eye-DEN-tih-fyd) Unrecognized or unknown.

weather balloon (WEH-thur buh-LOON) A tool used to look at weather.

wreckage (REK-ij) What is left of something after a crash.

Index

A
aliens, 15, 17, 19–21
Area 51, 20
Army, 8–10, 12–16, 18
autopsies, 17

B
Brazel, Mack, 6–8, 14

C
coffins, 15

D
Dennis, Glenn, 15–16

F
fire department, 18

H
Hangar 18, 19

M
Marcel, Major Jesse, 9, 11

R
Roswell, New Mexico, 4–6,
    18, 20

S
sheriff, 7–8

W
wreckage, 6–7, 10–11, 14,
    19–20

Web Sites

Due to the changing nature of Internet links, the Rosen Publishing Group, Inc., has developed an online list of Web sites related to the subject of this book. This site is updated regularly. Please use this link to access the list:
www.powerkidslinks.com/jgm/ufos/